One Wild Ember

The Prequel Novella to:

The Pyre Song Trilogy

Gisele Stein

ONE

Paddington Station swirls with the odour of old magic.

It's imperceptible to human senses, a concoction of ancient spells and simmering potions that has been stewing in London's underbelly for centuries. Yet, an alluring bouquet for any twenty-six-year-old witch eager to push the boundaries of her craft.

The moment the train door slides open, Sofia is beguiled.

A petite figure with a beehive of wild, raven locks, heavily lined eyes rimmed with smudged kohl, and a pout adorned with ruby red lipstick, she cuts an audacious silhouette in her slinky vintage dress and towering heels. Through oversized pink headphones, Nina Simone breathes words about a new dawn and a new day into her ears, and as the brass orchestra launches into the iconic chorus of "Feeling Good", Sofia steps into the city that awaits her with bated breath... or maybe that's just what she likes to imagine. She drops her bags with a heavy thud at her feet, lights a cigarette, and blows smoke in the air. Stretching, she reaches out her tattooed arms, sleeves of ink rippling with the movement, and lets her scent spread up and down the platform to attract a suitable carrier for her luggage.

Someone taps her on the shoulder, and she spins around with a soundless leopard snarl.

A young man in a conductor's uniform with neatly combed, mousy-brown hair and a firm expression, motions for her to remove her headphones. Sofia shifts the left ear cup just enough so she can hear the man lecture her.

"Miss, you can't smoke here."

Sofia gives him a glance the way one looks at the blackboard in detention. She blows smoke in his face.

"Instead of reprimanding me, darling, be a dear and carry my bags, why don't you? A gentleman would never leave a lady burdened with such heavy luggage." She ashes into his breast pocket, then turns on her heel and strides toward the exit.

"With pleasure, Miss," babbles the conductor,

suddenly all amenable. He hefts her bags from the ground and trails behind her like a faithful lapdog.

Sofia has sapped his willpower, rendering him pliant and eager to cater to her whims. A simple yet effective bit of magic: she is at the peak of her ovulation – an opportune time for any woman to attract attention. However, she amplified her appeal even further by casting a simple siphoning spell, leeching that magnetic essence from other females nearby. They might feel a twinge of fatigue, a bit of gloom for the rest of the day, but no lasting harm will befall them. That's how magic works: it's a constant give and take of energies, a delicate shuffle of nature's scales. Everything in the Universe is Anima, the spirit that flows through all living beings and inanimate objects alike. To wield magic, witches tap into this intricate web, manipulating the threads of Anima that connect all things. And to ignite a roaring blaze, sometimes one must first extinguish the flames of a dozen candles.

Heads turn as Sofia slices the crowd. Outside the station, London greets her with a stifling humidity that seems extreme even for mid-June. It's the fifteenth, and British summer in full swing, the city baking under a merciless sun that has prematurely browned Hyde Park to a sun-scorched expanse more akin to autumn.

It's not hard to guess which of the cars is waiting for

Sofia; she just has to look for the most expensive one. Today, it's a black Range Rover. Tinted windows. Polished metal. Commanding height.

The driver's door swings open. Out steps a woman in her early thirties, lithe and graceful with an instant aura of understated wit. Dark waves frame her features, complementing brown skin and eyes that sparkle with an intelligent, almost mischievous light. An anthracite jumpsuit hugs her athletic form – tasteful yet exuding an effortless sensuality.

Sofia saunters towards the Rover, the conductor trailing dutifully behind, clutching her bag like a lovesick teenager. As they near the car, he sidles up beside her.

"You know, Miss, I get off work soon." An uneasy smile. "Perhaps you'd allow me to take you out for a drink?"

Sofia smirks, revelling in the growing effects of her spell. She can sense the driver watching her with rapt fascination from the open car door. Which is why, with a subtle twitch of her fingers, Sofia amplifies the enchantment even further, her pheromones saturating the hot London air.

The conductor's eyes glaze over as her power takes deeper hold. "Or... or maybe you'd prefer to come back to my place instead?"

"Why, you daring thing…" Sofia runs a finger along his chin.

The conductor lets the bags slump to the ground. Now his hands reach for her waist. "I make a mean cheese toastie," he murmurs with a wonky grin.

But just as he's about to touch her, Sofia snaps her fingers again, which abruptly severs the spell. The young man blinks rapidly as reality reasserts itself. A whistle blows in the distance and his face drains of colour – the very train he's supposed to be working has just departed without him.

"Bon voyage, darling," Sofia coos as he scrambles away, cursing under his breath. She turns to the bemused driver. "Shall we, then?"

"Welcome back to the UK, Miss Guise," the woman says with a chuckle, opening the Rover's back door.

"Actually, the name's Hausmann," Sofia corrects her. "Or better yet, just call me Sofia."

"Oh, I'm sorry, Miss Haus… I mean, Sofia. I thought Mr Guise was your…"

"Everyone does, sweetheart. No need to fret your pretty head over it."

Guise (pronounced *goo-eeze*) is her foster father Mardequai's family name. Born in France sometime before the Fourth Crusade, he is one of the immortal druids who make up the other half of magical society alongside witches. A druid's aging process is substantially slowed – while a human or witch ages a year, a druid might only age something like a nanosecond. Conveniently, they also cannot be killed, thanks to a fortunate left-turn of their DNA. Immortality allows them to witness the gradual march of ages, and they pride themselves as the 'wardens of history.' Clearly, they're also practically drowning in modesty.

Instead of getting into the car, Sofia helps store her luggage in the boot – an unusually kind gesture for her, owed entirely to the fact that the driver is absolutely smoking.

"And who might you be?"

"I'm Pippa. Pippa Watson. I've been working for your father... I mean, for your, um... for Mr Guise here in London for five years."

"Five years? Wow, he must really trust you then."

Not enough to put her on the staff at Dunmorough though, Sofia adds silently. Sheltered in the Scottish Highlands, Dunmorough Castle is Mardequai's private sanctuary. Sofia has wandered those icy corridors since Mardequai took her in at age thirteen, right after the accident. Born in Germany, she's developed a strange mix of an accent since, somewhere between German and Scottish – now probably with slight East African undertones as well, thanks to this recent stretch abroad.

"I mean, I'd like to think so," Pippa replies, brushing a curl from her face.

She isn't a witch; Sofia can tell right off the bat. It's not that witches stand out, per se – they don't – but her excitement over Sofia's handling of the conductor was hard to miss. Pippa obviously hasn't seen much magic, let alone wields it herself.

Throughout history, the magical community has always intermingled with humans – out of sheer necessity to procreate, if for nothing else, given that witches are exclusively female and druids are so ancient that it's difficult to envision a fulfilling relationship with one. It does happen, but it's rare. Druids by and large have evolved beyond matters of love, let alone passion. They focus instead on grander matters, immersed in global politics and cunning schemes. To Sofia, there's nothing less appealing than a druid. They're like mouldy pieces of decade-old cheese – ancient, dry, and completely devoid of sex appeal.

Sofia slides into the plush rear cabin of the Rover, sinking into the soft leather seat. Pippa circles around and settles herself behind the wheel. With a purr of the engine, they glide away from Paddington Station and merge onto Bayswater Road.

"How was Chyulu Academy?" Pippa asks, effortlessly navigating rush hour.

"He told you about Chyulu, did he? So, you *have* earned your keep."

Either that, or she's under a particularly strong Whisperlock, the magical equivalent of an NDA, which turns a certain part of the mind into a vault. You can't put someone under a Whisperlock if they don't accept; they have to volunteer. But Sofia isn't particularly fond of the spell either way because sealing that vault requires the sacrifice of something valuable from the witch who casts it. To keep the balance, something must be given, maybe a cherished memory or a day in her lifespan, and, well, Sofia Hausmann is way too narcissistic to part easily with anything she holds dear.

Druids, while immortal, lack any inherent magical powers of their own, thus they rely on witches to perform such spells for them. Over the eons, this has naturally led them to become benefactors of the mystical arts. Living forever generally allows druids to amass vast fortunes, which they take pleasure in using to support and cultivate exceptionally talented witches. Mardequai stands out as perhaps the most notorious of these witch collectors – every witch in the UK (as well as a growing number from overseas) dreams of being affiliated with him. Mardequai is incredibly wealthy, wise beyond mortal comprehension, and wields tremendous influence across the globe; an invitation to join his inner circle is akin to receiving a knighthood in the magical realm. His patronage confers both prestige and access to unimaginable resources upon those he sponsors. Sofia grew up in his wealthy household, so is used to the opulent lifestyle that comes with being one of Mardequai's protégés. However, she also knows the strict discipline and sense of duty that's expected in return for such privileges.

He will not be pleased with her premature departure from Chyulu.

"Well, seeing as you know about the Academy, I take it you also know how it went for me," Sofia says, pouring herself a Laphroaig from the well-stocked minibar.

Pippa casts a guilty glance through the rear mirror as she turns onto Park Lane, leaving Marble Arch behind.

"Go on then, what did he tell you?"

"He said you got expelled for unruly conduct, but he didn't go into more detail."

"And you would like me to go into more detail now, wouldn't you?"

"I would like to take you to your new home in the city now," Pippa replies dutifully.

Liar. Her curiosity is palpable, her thirst for juicy details about Sofia's misadventures in higher education practically radiating off her in waves.

The Chyulu Academy of Higher Witchery, nestled

deep in the cloud forests of the Chyulu Hills in southern Kenya, stands as the pinnacle of magical education and governance. The roots of witchcraft stretch back to the dawn of humanity in the Great Rift Valley, and African magical bloodlines are considered the strongest and most refined. It's for this reason that the Academy is revered across the world. It isn't merely a university; it's the gateway to the echelons of magical politics. Admission is highly competitive, reserved for those who demonstrate exceptional skill in the foundational aspects of witchcraft – or those who know the right people. Students at Chyulu Academy engage in advanced studies under the tutelage of some of the most accomplished witches and druids from around the globe. The curriculum is rigorous and expansive, focusing on the mastery of intricate spells and ancient enchantments, as well as the more subtle art of diplomacy.

For the three years Sofia lasted in the perpetual mountain mist, she was bored out of her mind. No wonder she snapped in the end and set the library ablaze during an illicit late-night spell experiment. The fire raged for hours, reducing centuries of priceless scripts and scrolls to smouldering ash. Though she claimed it was an accident (which it wasn't), the Elders saw it as a brash act of disrespect for the academy's treasured repositories of knowledge (which it was). Her raw talent is prodigious, no question there, but her inability to exercise restraint and discipline became a problem, to say the least. Really, she did them a favour; they had been looking for a reason to get rid of her for months.

A half hour later, Pippa steers the car onto a quiet Belgravia street, pulling up before an immaculately preserved townhouse that exudes old money opulence from every shiny white brick and every perfectly tended window box.

Sofia has only been here once before, during her brief stopover on the way to Kenya three years prior. Though she'd pestered Mardequai incessantly to tag along on his jaunts to the city, he'd always refused. Instead, she grew up cloistered and home-tutored at Dunmorough, a sheltered upbringing which, naturally, only stoked an insatiable craving for the forbidden thrills she imagined pulsed through London's streets. She'd sown her wild oats travelling the globe for a while before Mardequai called her back to start at Chyulu, though. And now the city of London is ready to be taken by storm, at last.

Sofia follows Pippa into the grand townhouse, their heels clacking on the marble floor of the entrance hall.

"He hasn't come back from his meeting with the Druid Council," Pippa explains, "but he requested you wait for him in his study." She shoots Sofia a coy smile over her shoulder as she leads the way down a corridor lined with curated art pieces and expensive antiquities.

As they enter the study, Sofia can't resist placing her hand on the doorframe right next to Pippa's face. "Sure you don't want to... keep me company while we wait?"

Pippa bites her lip, her eyes gleaming. She's clearly tickled by the flattery. "I'm afraid there are other matters he asked me to take care of." And with a wink, she excuses herself, leaving Sofia wanting amid old books.

She wanders aimlessly through Mardequai's library, trails her fingers along the spines of ancient tomes, meanders between the towering mahogany shelves.

A gilded invitation lying on the large oak desk catches her eye. She scoops it up, instantly recognising the ornate insignia embossed on the parchment – the Global Assembly of Arcane Guardians, the GAAG, convenes regularly to bring together the world's most powerful druids and witches. Over the course of two weeks, participants discuss a topic of relevance, and this year's gathering promises to be particularly spicy:

The honoured elders of the Global Assembly of Arcane Guardians request the privilege of your esteemed presence at the two-hundred-and-fifteenth convening to commune on the matter of Magic's role in restoring the Earth.

This year, we shall delve into the urgent need to harness Anima to reverse the devastation wrought by human folly upon our realm. As per the two-hundred-and-seventh referendum, ICAG-registered witches and druids voted in favour of a magical reveal to guide humanity onto a path of environmental renewal and atonement. This reveal will be presented to the respective heads of state during the Global Summit on Climate Action in London this September.

The purpose of the assembly is to ensure a smooth transition for this unprecedented revelation, and to gather in the city of London to show a united front.

The grand opening ceremony shall be held at the sacred...

Sofia's eyes quickly scan the rest of the invitation, noting the logistical details before setting the parchment back down on the desk. The recent referendum held by the international magical community was a historic vote to determine whether witches and druids would reveal their existence to the human world. The International Council of Arcane Governance (ICAG) mandated that every registered witch and druid cast their vote on this monumental decision. Sofia voted in favour of revela-tion. However, she chose to keep that a secret from

Mardequai. Though he never explicitly stated his opinion on the matter (he never states his opinion on *anything*), she has a strong suspicion that her foster father holds a differing viewpoint. Mardequai, with his centuries of wisdom and deep-rooted connection to the old ways, likely favours maintaining the separation between the magical and human realms.

But despite the opposition from traditionalists like Mardequai, the referendum passed, albeit by a narrow margin. The magical world now finds itself on the brink of a new era, tasked with the challenge of preparing for the inevitable merger with human society. Centuries of secrecy and mistrust will need to be overcome, and the magical community will have to brave the clash with human politics, science, not to mention religion.

Naturally, Sofia is just in it for the fun, really. She's done hiding.

"I hear the Kenyan climate didn't agree with you any longer."

She whirls around at the sound of Mardequai's gravelly voice. He stands framed in the library doorway; an imposing figure clad in a charcoal suit tailored from fine wool. Despite his advanced age he holds himself with ramrod straight posture.

"You got yourself expelled from the Academy, I take it?" To Sofia's surprise, Mardequai's eyes crinkle with amusement rather than admonishment. "To be honest, I never expected you to last as long as you did up there."

Sofia opens her mouth to protest, but Mardequai waves a hand. "No, no, don't try to explain it away, child. I'm delighted, really." He chuckles. "Had you not taken matters into your own hands, I would have summoned you home from Chyulu myself."

"You... would have?" Sofia sputters, dumbfounded. "Why?"

"Because your true education lies elsewhere." Mardequai crosses the room towards her. "You possess rare talents, Sofia – talents that risk being squandered behind those dusty academy walls..."

He settles into an armchair by the fireplace, motioning for Sofia to join him.

"Then why did you go out of your way to get me accepted in the first place?"

"I had my reasons," Mardequai replies, his voice laced with enigmatic calm. Not a trace of his French origins clings to his accent – he sounds as quintessentially English as the Windsors. When Sofia first encountered him years ago, he addressed her in impeccable German as well. Over the ensuing years, she discovered he also commands fluent Italian, Spanish, and Mandarin with equal ease. And while this mastery of languages is remarkable, it's less surprising considering his age. After all, the man is over eight hundred years old. If there's one thing Mardequai has in abundance – besides his riches, perhaps – it is time.

A silence falls between them, thick as fog and just as opaque. It lingers, suffocating the room until, as usual, Sofia is the one to break it.

"So, what can I do for you?" she asks. "Your message said you had a job for me here in London."

"Not a job, exactly. More like a... fun pastime over the summer."

Sofia arches an eyebrow. "What, you want me to pick up knitting?"

"I would like you to make a name for yourself."

"Doing what exactly?"

"The same sort of mischief that got you ousted from the Academy."

Sofia blinks. "You want me burning down the British Library?"

"By summer's end, I want the entire magical community of London utterly enthralled by your... reputation." A wry smile plays across Mardequai's lips. "What means you employ to get there are up to you."

Sofia squints as if trying to adjust her eyes to bright light. It's not an unusual request, per se. Mardequai's protégés regularly carry out tasks, run errands, gather intelligence for him. But after her sheltered upbringing, this blatant invitation to run rampant strikes her as a little strange, out of character. Suspicious, even.

"Why?" she asks simply.

Mardequai rises and walks toward the window. "Because, my tempestuous child," he begins, crossing his arms behind his back, "it is about time you and I stepped out of the shadows and showed the world out there what we are made of." He turns back toward her, eyes glinting.

Sofia holds his gaze a beat. "So, how will *you* show them?"

The sly smile returns, a warning that she over-stepped. Clearly, his aims are none of her concern. Another weighty pause, then: "Well, I best be on my way." And just like that, Mardequai makes to leave. That's another thing about him: he is never one to linger. Sofia's life under his roof lacks nothing in terms of material comforts – quite the opposite – yet he's far from a father figure. A distant uncle at best, around but perpetually aloof.

"So, these means for making my name?" Sofia calls after him.

"Yes?"

"How above-board must they be, legally speaking?"

Mardequai pauses. "Magical law is absolute."

"And what about human law?"

He turns back around. "Deer may set paths in the

forest, but that doesn't mean the wolves will follow them."

Sofia smiles contentedly. This is getting better and better.

"Say, this wouldn't have anything to do with the GAAG, now, would it?" she asks, draping her legs casually over the armrest.

"All will be revealed in due course, my dear. Don't you worry about anything but your task for the time being," replies Mardequai, his expression giving nothing away. "Now, I will be in and out of London over the summer, but the house is all yours, and Pippa is always at your disposal. Anything you need, she will take care of it. Oh, and Sofia?"

"Yeah?"

"Do not disappoint me."

And with a click of the latch, Mardequai is out the door, leaving Sofia alone, her eyes glinting with mischief.

"...Anything I need, huh?"

Sofia presses Pippa against the kitchen door with reckless abandon, pouring Don Julio into her mouth straight from the bottle. The tequila dribbles down Pippa's chin, and Sofia leans in, licking the trail like a vampire licks blood, savouring both the liquor and the soft whimpers escaping Pippa's lips. Their bodies crash together in a heated frenzy, hands desperately tugging at clothes until they fall to the floor. Sofia lifts Pippa onto the counter, trailing kisses down her neck, across her collar bone, her chest, lower still until... until... *until...*

———

The two women lie tangled on the kitchen floor, chests heaving and skin glistening with a sheen of sweat in the moonlight coming in from the glass roof.

"So, what's your story, if you don't mind me asking?" Pippa murmurs, tracing patterns across Sofia's stomach. "You mentioned at the station your last name wasn't Guise, but Hausmann...?"

Sofia's expression clouds briefly. "Mardequai is my foster father. He took me in after I lost my family at thirteen."

"What happened?" Pippa asks, barely above a whisper.

"Car accident. That's how I got this." Sofia holds up her left arm where an angry red scar winds up from her knuckles to her elbow, now incorporated into an elaborate snake tattoo. "Never felt as useless as I felt that night."

"What do you mean?"

"I couldn't help them. I made it out, but I failed to save my parents and my… sister." Her voice constricts ever so slightly on the last word.

"You had a sister?"

"A twin. Her name was Alva." Sofia offers a smile, but it's tinged with sadness. "Can you imagine the pandemonium we would have caused if she was still alive today?"

"Double trouble," Pippa chuckles. "You two were close, I take it?"

Sofia pours herself another tequila.

Pippa nods like that was answer enough. "Well, you must miss her terribly."

Swirling the liquid in her glass, Sofia falls silent for a heavy moment. The loss still cuts deep, a wound that refuses to scab over. "Losing her left avoid you couldn't begin to comprehend," she says and tosses back the tequila in one burning swallow.

"I guess it all makes sense now," notes Pippa.

"What does?"

"Everything I've heard about you."

"Which is what?"

Pippa rolls over, kissing her on the shoulder. "That you can be rash," she says, lips brushing against Sofia's inked skin. "A little… unhinged even? But that there's probably no other young witch working harder on her craft than you are."

"And that makes sense to you now *because*...?"

"Because you obviously believe that power and control are the only means to prevent any more tragedy or loss in your life. If you become powerful enough, you won't have to experience that pain, that helplessness ever again."

"I'm that see-through, am I?"

"Not see-through, exactly... just, you know, *human*."

"I'm many things, darling, but I'm most certainly not just human."

Sofia rises, sits on the countertop, and lights a cigarette, allowing for the energy in the room to shift. It's time to get moving.

"Well, I'm pretty sure this was a breach of my contract," Pippa laughs nervously, breaking the silence she clearly recognises as an awkward one. She covers her bare chest with her jumpsuit and gets up as well, stroking Sofia's thigh.

"Don't worry," Sofia replies, picking a bit of tobacco from her tongue. "You'll have forgotten all about it as soon as you leave this room."

"What? Hang on, you put a forgetting spell on me? – No way! I would have... like... *noticed* that."

"That's exactly what you said after the first time."

"You've done this to me *before*?"

"And *that's* what you said after the second. Now, if you'll excuse me" – Sofia drops her cigarette into the Don Julio bottle and slides off the counter in one fluid motion – "I have to get ready."

"Get ready? For what?"

"I'm going out."

"But it's two in the morning."

Sofia seizes her by the waist and captures her lover's lips in one last searing kiss. "Just in time for witching hour," she whispers against Pippa's neck. "Do some research, will you, darling? Find me a high-profile event where I can cause a deliciously scandalous scene tonight." Sofia trails a fingertip along Pippa's jawline as she ponders. "As for transportation, the Range Rover is a bit too understated for the occasion, don't you think? Feel free to pick something a little more... ostentatious. And you might want to sober up a bit; we're leaving in half an hour."

With that, Sofia disentangles herself, snatching up her dress and heels before striding out of the kitchen and through the servant's quarter in all her naked glory.

Two

Nothing embodies rampant chaos quite like a tiger raised in captivity, tasting freedom for the first time in the wild. Devoid of any hunting skills or necessary caution, the tiger becomes a paradox of aggression and naïveté. It is as unaware of the threats lurking as it is untouched by the rules of the jungle, and so its actions become both unpredictable and fraught with peril. The tiger, driven by a blinding hunger, confronts the wilderness with dangerous and unguarded fervour.

The moment her gilded cage is opened, Sofia bursts forth with a feral abandon that knows no bounds.

That night, in her lavish bedroom suite, the plush chaise longue is strewn with discarded silk robes and lace negligees as she reclines amid rumpled satin sheets.

Ornate tapestries and a giant canopy bed lend an air of opulence to the boudoir. The air is heavy with the scent of jasmine from a flower bouquet on her vanity, mingling with the smoke of freshly lit incense sticks.

Smartphone in hand, she taps out a new Instagram handle – 'mypinkcauldron' – and opens the camera. A teasing smile plays across her lips as she sets the ambiance with a tap of her fingers, bathing the room in a sultry pink light.

Clad in nothing but black lacy undergarments that leave little to the imagination, Sofia begins filming a 'get ready with me' video as the White Stripes' iconic riff to "Seven Nation Army" thumps in the background. With a subtle hand gesture, her makeup- and mascara brushes levitate in a mesmerising orbit around her face, applying foundation, eyeshadow, and liner with magical precision as she lip-syncs the lyrics, resting witch face and all.

Once fully done up in smouldering makeup, Sofia jumps onto the bed and begins an uninhibited dance around the bedroom, smartphone still filming, each sway of her hips and toss of her hair more alluring than the last as she moves to the raw beat.

She posts the video with a simple caption ('witches be like...'), then rummages through the immense closet, which seems to contain a motley selection of Mardequai's castoffs. Because she didn't bring any party clothes (and because not even Pippa Watson can sidestep Harrods's peasant opening hours), she settles for one of the druid's black suit jackets that drapes around her petite frame like a boyfriend's oversized blazer. Tossing it on over her lacy underthings, she completes the look with a pair of stilettos. Then she sweeps out into the sultry London night.

In the driveway, a scarlet red original Aston Martin awaits, Pippa leaning against the gleaming flanks, arms crossed.

"Will this do?" she asks, eyebrow cocked.

Sofia's lips curve into a wicked grin. "Just," she purrs.

"So, I have found you a movie premiere for tonight," Pippa announces, now behind the steering wheel. The forgetting spell has clearly worked on her. While she still remembers her assignment, it has completely slipped her mind that she and Sofia were knocking over spice racks and condiments in a passionate embrace less than an hour ago. "Damian Arknight's new cyberpunk thriller *Neon Kill* had its red-carpet gala earlier tonight. The after-party is still on at an abandoned train station in Shoreditch."

"Perfect."

Arknight is one of the hottest directors in Hollywood at the moment, his sci-fi epics repeatedly smashing box office records.

"Obviously, you're not on the list," Pippa says with a smirk. "But I didn't figure that would stop you."

Sofia, sitting next to Pippa, connects her phone to the discreetly integrated Bluetooth system and soon after, David Bowie's "Cat People" fills the car with its gritty vibe. She catches Pippa's approving smirk in the mirror, face illuminated by the city lights flashing by. As the chorus erupts with gasoline, both of their bodies can't keep it in any longer and start to move – Sofia ecstatically, Pippa with the most subtle of shoulder rolls, which is so damn sexy it almost unravels the witch in her passenger seat.

To distract herself, Sofia checks her freshly minted Instagram reel, content to notice the dizzying metrics pouring in. With the help of a little magical tweak, thousands of views, likes, and new followers have amassed in mere minutes, and comments flood the feed:

Who is this goddess?

I'd risk it all for one night with her!!!

How did she make the brushes float like that? Some kind of special effect??

The editing in this is insane, I need to know how it was done!

The latter comments hint at a very obvious breach of

magical laws banning revelation of magic to humans. But Sofia's video straddles that line skilfully, and with modern film editing so mind-bending, just enough doubt lingers. Besides, the Reveal is imminent – what does it matter now? A sly grin spreads as she hits record on an Instagram Live video.

"Well, well, well... look who's waltzed onto the A-list tonight for Damian Arknight's premiere. Maybe I'll snag the lead in his next erotic thriller..."

The streets of Shoreditch throb with bass as the Aston's engine announces their arrival. Pippa brings the ride to a stop and Sofia weaves her fingers in an intricate gesture, renewing the siphoning spell she used at Paddington Station earlier.

Stepping out onto the red carpet, she's an entrancing vision in Mardequai's oversized blazer and those skyscraper stilettos. A palpable hush falls over the crowd as every eye and every camera lens turns towards her. Though no one can explain the gravitational pull, the flashes begin popping in a frenzy, photographers jostling for the best angles as Sofia struts past them.

At the entrance, the doorman's jaw goes momentarily slack before he recovers with a wolfish grin. "Name's not on the list, love."

Sofia leans in close, trailing a fingertip along his clipboard. In a subtle twisting of reality, his pupils blow wide, transfixed.

"I'm quite certain it is," she murmurs, the barest caress of enchantment nudging his perception.

"Ya... yeah, of course," he rumbles, then ushers her inside.

Sofia slinks into the throbbing depths of the train-station-turned-nightclub, and the thunder of bass reverberates through her bones. She wastes no time in making Mardequai proud. Extending her senses outward, she taps into the energy surrounding her – the heat of dancing bodies and the electric charge of the pulsing lights – to fuel her next spell. First, a slight tweak of the music: Sofia's obsessed with all the icons from the sixties to the nineties – Dylan. Bowie. Joplin. Nicks. Cobain. She might also throw the occasional indie rock classic into the mix; modern mainstream music, however, leaves her cold (aside from Taylor Swift and Florence and the Machine, naturally). So, she draws a subtle thread of energy from the swirling neon lights to change the track to The Clash's "Should I Stay or Should I Go." Then, with a graceful gesture, she redirects this harvested energy to manipulate the room. This causes every soul gyrating on the dance floor to unconsciously copy her movements in perfect synchronicity. She's like a puppet master, pulling threads at will, each step and sway a mirror of her own.

Sofia begins her dance routine (elaborately choreographed over years alone at Dunmorough), her hips swaying as the crowd follows her lead like an unholy dance troupe, creating a flashmob. The spell has taken full effect now. Hundreds of eyes lock onto her at the front, while ushered voices from the sidelines trade murmurs of awed speculation. "Who is that?" "I've never seen her before..."

When the final chords echo through the club, the crowd's frenzy subsides into applause and scattered cheers. Sofia gracefully bows, then releases her dancers from the spell and excuses herself from the dance floor.

On her way to reapply her lipstick in the bathroom, she brushes past a heated discussion between a young woman and a man whose demeanour, despite his fancy suit, still screams 'used car salesman.' Sofia instantly recognises the woman from the movie posters. It's Mia Bennett, the actor starring in Arknight's new film. And the man is none other than David Voss, a notoriously sleazy London club-owner who has skirted British high society for decades, making regular appearances on the cover of *The Sun* or the *Daily Mirror*, though usually as a plus one of someone actually famous. No doubt he's organised *this* soiree as well.

"Remember who made you a star, you little tart?" he sneers now, grabbing Mia's wrist as she attempts to pull away. "You think you're too good for me now?"

Before Sofia can intervene, Voss seizes Mia by the shoulders and mashes his lips against hers in a brutish facsimile of a kiss. Mia squirms against his grasp, panicked eyes finding Sofia's over Voss's shoulder.

Sofia stalks toward them, power thrumming through her veins. "I do believe the lady said no."

Voss releases Mia, who takes the opportunity to bolt towards the restrooms. He turns to face Sofia. "And who the bloody hell are y—"

But before he can fully voice the challenge, a peculiar green tinge creeps up his neck and his expression contorts. An invisible force seems to clench his stomach into knots as nausea visibly washes over him. He doubles over, retching violently into a silver ice bucket.

Sofia watches with clinical detachment as the brute is laid low by her subtle hex. "You want to be more careful with the canapés next time, darling," she whispers in his ear once he's done. "Some of them are delicate affairs – mistreat them, and they retaliate in kind." She straightens his lapels while he wipes his mouth. Then she turns on her heel and follows Mia into the bathroom.

Inside, a shaken Mia Bennett hunches on the

counter, blotting away stray tears with a wad of tissue paper. For the moment, they are the only occupants.

"I'm so sorry you had to see that," Mia whimpers, hugging her knees.

"I'm sorrier still that you had to endure it." Sofia takes a seat beside her. "That creep had no right to put his hands on you."

Mia manages a smile. "Except he... he kind of... does. You see, he's the one who got me started in the business. Took me under his wing, you could say."

"Well, even if that's true," Sofia states firmly, "you earned that lead role through your own talents, pet. He may have opened the door, but you walked through it yourself, now, didn't you?"

Mia's eyes widen, a hint of confidence blossoming in their depths. "I... I did, didn't I?"

Sofia shrugs, applying a fresh layer of lipstick.

"Thank you... I... I really needed to hear that tonight." Mia worries her lip. "Say, did... did you want to get a drink or something?"

Sofia leans in so close their noses almost touch. "It would be my absolute pleasure, gorgeous. Lead the way."

Back inside the club, Mia makes a beeline for the velvet rope cordoning off the VIP section, dozens of smartphone cameras instantly trained on her every stride.

David Voss unhitches the rope as she nears, openly leering.

"What took you so long? Got someone important I need you to... *charm*," he murmurs, hand drifting down to grope her backside.

As Sofia attempts to follow Mia inside, Voss blocks her path with an upraised palm. "A-listers only." He sneers at Sofia's DIY blazer ensemble.

"Then what are *you* doing in here?" Sofia retorts, the quip echoing through the room just as another song ends.

A wave of raucous laughter erupts from the VIP crowd. Even Mia's co-star, action hero Marshall Grayson, cracks up and high-fives the ballsy intruder. "She got you good there, Davey-boy!"

Voss flushes a mottled crimson, lips quivering with rage. But just as he opens his mouth, Sofia discreetly casts yet another subtle spell with one finger.

Voss's pupils blow wide for the span of a heartbeat before he staggers, eyes crossing. A steady stream of drool leaks from the corner of his slack jaw, soaking through his tie as he crosses his legs over.

"Oh...oh, God..." Voss whimpers, swaying on his feet.

"Voss, did you just... shit yourself?" remarks Grayson, now holding up his own phone.

Roaring laughter erupts. Voss turns and half-runs, half-waddles away. "Y-you did this!" he just about manages to hiss over his shoulder, glaring at Sofia.

"Well, it appears a spot just opened up on the VIP list," she declares and without waiting for an invitation, saunters through the velvet ropes and makes for the bar. Catching the bartender's eye, she states loud enough for all to hear, "I'll have a bottle of your finest, most disgracefully overpriced champagne, please. I hear it's on David Voss's tab tonight."

Another roar of cheers meets her declaration as she's passed an outrageously extravagant bottle. Popping the cork with a theatrical flourish, Sofia pours a glass and raises the fizzing flute high.

"To breaking free of overgrown man-children and realising our true worth, witches!" She knocks back the entire glass, champagne fizzing down her throat. The revellers erupt into celebration, all cameras now trained on her.

For this tiger, the night is just getting started.

THREE

Pippa enters the bedroom without so much as a courtesy knock.

It has taken less than two months for the boundaries between personal assistant and... well, whatever Sofia is, to dissipate entirely. She carries a silver tray laden with Sofia's usual morning indulgences – a ruby red grapefruit half, fresh-squeezed orange juice, buttered toast soldiers, and a coffee grande noir that dwarfs any mortal mug. Five weeks have elapsed since the fateful movie premiere that kicked off Sofia's meteoric rise to fame, and she has kept busy since.

"You're *The Sun*'s cover girl this fine morning," Pippa announces, placing the tray on the nightstand together with the fresh newspaper. "There are three photographers lurking in the hedges, so do try to avoid flashing them from the windows again, please? Oh, and Rihanna left you a DM. She wants to 'hang' the next time she's in London."

And that's just the least of it: in a mere month, Sofia has amassed over a million Instagram followers, become a permanent presence in the gossip pages, and cultivated an entourage of powerful, young witches all clamouring for her approval – including Celeste Devereaux of the venerable Devereaux coven, clairvoyant darling Minnie Allen, and former child prodigy Saskia Antonov.

"Amy..." comes Sofia's muffled groan from beneath the sheets.

Pippa rolls her eyes. "My name is Pippa, not Amy."

"Play... Amy..."

With a put-upon sigh, Pippa thumbs the stereo, filling the boudoir with the opening strains of Amy Winehouse's "Help Yourself." Another morning ritual.

Sofia's tousled crown finally emerges, bleary eyes lined with last night's smudged mascara, reeling from yet another decadent night painting the town pink. She sips her coffee as Pippa parts the curtains, the paparazzi's flashes popping outside.

"You look rather ravishing this morning."

"That's because I'm looking at you, gorgeous," Sofia murmurs. Despite the ease of being able to erase any awkward encounters from Pippa's memory, she hasn't so much as stolen a kiss from her PA since that first heated tryst in the kitchen. Though she'll never admit it aloud, she has grown rather... fond of sweet Pippa, with her crooked smiles and hidden depths. Too fond for such casual dalliances.

Sofia turns her attention to *The Sun*'s gossip pages, the headline blaring:

*WHO THE F*** IS 'MYPINKCAULDRON'? MYSTERIOUS SOCIALITE TAKES LONDON BY STORM!*

The article breathlessly chronicles this enigmatic influencer's rise to notoriety:

In a mere month, the bombshell known only as 'mypinkcauldron' has reached over a million Instagram followers and become the talk of every A-list event in the city. Her true identity remains a mystery, but one thing is certain: this vixen knows how to make an entrance and leave chaos in her wake!

Nightclub impresario David Voss has made no secret of his seething grudge against the siren after she publicly humiliated him at the premiere of Neon Kill *last month. This past Saturday, Voss brazenly refused entry to Mypinkcauldron and her entourage at his exclusive Soho hotspot, The Sapphire Lounge – including starlet Mia Bennett, who allegedly dumped Voss after his VIP lounge debacle.*

One has to wonder why the ladies even deigned to grace Voss's club. But then, Mypinkcauldron seems to court controversy wherever she goes. Whether she's inciting a champagne-fuelled food fight at The Wolseley or frolicking topless in the Trafalgar Square fountains, this mischief-maker knows how to scandalise high society – and somehow get away unscathed!

Pippa clears her throat pointedly. "Mr Guise is in the country. He requests your presence at Cliveden House this afternoon."

The Sun's pages flutter to the floor as Sofia drinks in the sight of her assistant, all pert professionalism.

"A jaunt to the countryside, how positively pastoral!" Sofia perks up. "Pack your bikini, Pippa darling. We'll go a little early and make a day of it! I hear their pool is divine."

Pippa fixes her with a look. "...And allow the country mice a glimpse of my knickers? – I think not."

Bloody hell, what a woman.

———

On the drive to Cliveden House, Pippa broaches the subject of Sofia's burgeoning notoriety.

"Listen, I know it's not my place," she begins, "but I worry about the potential fallout from all these... let's call them 'high-spirited' evenings you've been indulging in."

Sofia arches a brow, lips quirking. She's opted for the passenger seat today, mainly just to vex Pippa. "Worried for my virtue, are we?"

Pippa huffs, cheeks pinking. "More for the long-term consequences to your reputation. The tabloids are having a field day branding you as some sort of debauched party girl."

"Well, all publicity is good publicity, or so I'm told," Sofia replies airily.

Pippa's expression softens, concern etching her brow. "I just... I'd hate to see you reduced to some gossip rag caricature. I know there is more to you."

Sofia reaches over to pat Pippa's thigh, a frisson of electricity sparking at the innocent touch. "You're terribly sweet to fret, darling, but I assure you I'm a big girl. I can handle my liquor and my reputation in equal measure."

Pippa subsides into silence as the car wends its way towards the sprawling country estate.

Cliveden House looms ahead, a majestic Italianate mansion set amidst immaculate grounds and formal gardens. Mardequai frequently utilises the estate when his business brings him down south, as it offers an unparalleled combination of privacy and opulence.

Much like Dunmorough, Cliveden provides a secure and luxurious retreat where he can conduct his affairs without prying eyes or unwanted interruptions. The grandeur of the surroundings serves as a testament to his power and influence, setting the stage for whatever important matters he wishes to discuss. It's fair to assume Sofia is not the only guest he's expecting to meet here today.

After a leisurely dip in the outdoor pool (which Pippa staunchly declined to join), Sofia towels off, and the pair ventures inside.

Upon hearing they're part of Mardequai's entourage, the concierge escorts them into a sumptuous conference room, all rich mahogany wainscoting and floor-to-ceiling windows overlooking the gardens. The table is set up for a luncheon of five. Fine bone china gleams in the soft chandelier light, each place setting adorned with polished silverware.

"I don't think you'll be in *this* meeting," notes Pippa with a nod at the table set up. "I'm supposed to bring you to the Library Bar."

Sofia hops up to perch on the edge of the table, crossing her legs with deliberate provocation as she studies Pippa. "And how are you planning on doing that, puppet?"

"Well, I was thinking of employing my irresistible

charm. But if that fails, there's always the option of rolling you up in one of these fancy rugs and smuggling you out like a burrito."

Sofia barks out a laugh, shaking her head. "Don't worry, your charm will always suffice to move me, Pippa Watson."

She slides off the table, her amusement fading into something more thoughtful. Running a hand through her hair, she turns to face the window, her reflection ghostly in the glass.

After a moment of silence, she speaks again, her voice softer now. "About what you said in the car earlier... Do you really believe there's more to me?"

Pippa quirks a smile. "Well, you're certainly more than just a pretty face. You also happen to have an impeccable taste in vintage Amy Winehouse records."

Sofia huffs out a laugh, but her eyes remain earnest, searching. Pippa sobers, moving to stand before her. "Of course, I believe there's more to you. Look at you, you're brilliant, and passionate, and so... so full of life."

Something raw and aching flickers across Sofia's features then, her usual sarcasm stripped away. Slowly, she reaches out to twine her fingers with Pippa's. "I'm not sure I think of myself that way," she confesses, barely a whisper.

Pippa squeezes her hand. "That's because you're too

busy being the Patron Saint of Mischief and Bollocks all the time," she jokes, and they both laugh.

And then, as if magnetised, they're gravitating towards each other, lips meeting in a soft brush that swiftly deepens into something hungrier. Pippa makes a small sound of protest even as she tangles her fingers in Sofia's hair, pressing closer.

"No, we can't, not here..."

"Shhh, don't think," Sofia murmurs against her mouth, nipping at Pippa's bottom lip as her hands slide beneath the hem of her shirt.

They lose themselves in the heated push and pull. The distant click of approaching footsteps in the corridor goes unnoticed, and it's only when Mardequai's unmistakable baritone reaches their ears that they spring apart, flushed and panting, frantically righting dishevelled clothing. Giggling like naughty schoolgirls, they scurry out onto the balcony to hide just as the dining room doors swing inwards.

A procession of British magical society's most elite files inside, taking their seats at the table.

Sofia recognises key players amongst the gathering. The druid Ambrose Hudspeth, rumoured to own half the Premier League teams. Silas Pierson, another druid and media magnate with controlling interests in Sky News. Orna Morrígan, the flame-haired witch credited with hexing several heads of state during the Cold War. And Catherine Delargy, who allegedly ensorcelled the London Stock Exchange in an attempt to take down Big Pharma in the nineties.

"Shouldn't we...?" Pippa whispers, her eyes darting towards the conference room.

Sofia responds with an almost imperceptible shake of her head, pressing a finger to her lips. Whatever matters have drawn this assembly together, they're undoubtedly of immense importance. Sofia leans in closer, straining to catch every word.

Mardequai presides at the head of the table. Once everyone has taken their seats, he begins to speak, his voice measured yet with an undercurrent of urgency. "My esteemed companions, I have called this gathering because, as you know, we stand on the precipice of a monumental change, one that will shape the course of our future. With the GAAG fast approaching, it is imperative that we present a united front. I trust that everyone here shares my conviction: revealing the true extent of our powers and ancient wisdom to the mortal world will be a grave error, with far-reaching, catastrophic consequences."

From their hidden vantage point on the balcony, Sofia can't help but huff out a silent laugh at the two notions druids *always* feel compelled to emphasise when speaking of witch power: one, druids' monopoly on age-old wisdom, and two, their immortality. Witches, on the other hand, never feel the need to assert their own importance. Their power is self-evident, and everyone, including the druids, is well aware of it.

Catherine Delargy speaks up. "Your wisdom on this matter is, of course, beyond reproach, Mardequai. The risks are undeniable, and we'd be fools to think otherwise. However, if I may play devil's advocate for a moment, in light of the escalating ecological crisis, might it not be prudent to reveal ourselves to humanity? With nature being ravaged at an unprecedented pace, our guidance could be invaluable in steering them towards a more sustainable path. I, for one, am starting to notice my powers shift as Anima becomes harder and harder to wield."

"Maybe it's time to brush up on your basics then, rather than exposing all of us to human folly," interjects Orna Morrígan, a vicious smile tugging at the corners of her mouth. "Anima has always been a fickle mistress. It takes true skill to navigate her whims."

Catherine breathes in sharply, but Silas Pierson interferes before the two witches can quarrel. "And need we remind you of the calamitous consequences the last time your kind chose to expose themselves against druid advice? The repercussions threatened not only our own community but the very fabric of the world itself."

Orna's eyes cloud, her tone now grave. "Our German ancestors were deceived by the Third Reich's promises of power and respect, I believe this with all my heart. Naively, they thought they could manipulate the Nazi regime to further their own agenda. Instead, it was the witches who were ruthlessly exploited, their sacred magic perverted to serve Hitler's twisted ambitions. It was a grievous error in judgment, one that was paid for in blood and tears. But surely, we have grown wiser from the harsh lessons of the past?"

"I beg to differ, Orna," Mardequai counters, his voice taking on a deeper tone. "I beg to differ. For us druids, the errors of the past are not easily forgotten, nor should they be. Regardless, the damage is done. The vote has been cast. However, the upcoming assembly offers us a singular chance to chart a new course. One that many in this room have long believed to be our only viable path forward. Cooperation with humans has proven futile; it is time we consider a bolder strategy. The mortals have strayed too far from the path of wisdom, and mere words will no longer suffice to guide them back. They must be shown the way, with a firm and unyielding hand."

He pauses, letting his words settle. "Consider this,

the combined might of witchcraft and druid wisdom has always been unparalleled. If we seized control of the reins, no human force could stand against us. We could steer the course of entire nations, reshape the foundations of society under our enlightened rule. The world would be healed, the balance restored. And we would emerge as the rightful stewards of this earth, guiding humanity towards a brighter future, even if they must be dragged to it kicking and screaming. It is not a path for the faint of heart, but I ask you: do we not owe it to ourselves, to the generations to come, to take this leap? To forge a new order in which magic and wisdom reign supreme?"

"With all due respect, Mardequai," interjects Ambrose Hudspeth, "what you propose is nothing short of a far-fetched fantasy. Such a plan could never come to fruition. It would require the unanimous consent of the entire international magical community. Need I remind you of the Concordat of the First Elders? The agreement explicitly forbids any attempt at interference with mortal affairs on such a scale. We would need – well – another referendum is what we'd need, and it would never pass."

Mardequai remains unperturbed. "Ah, but agreements are not set in stone, my dear Ambrose. They can be amended or even abandoned if the need arises. More to the point, we need not secure the support of every coven and council across the globe. What we require is a coalition of the willing, a core group of committed and powerful allies united in purpose and in resolve."

Out on the balcony, Sofia and Pippa exchange a look of wide-eyed disbelief, barely daring to breathe lest they be discovered. Pippa mouths silently, "Is he serious?"

But Sofia's features remain blank.

Her heart nearly stops when Mardequai strides towards the window, his foot landing mere inches from their hiding spot. Sofia flattens herself against the wall, pulling Pippa flush against her as they hold their breath.

"Over the past few weeks, I have been engaged in extensive travels, meeting with long-standing friends and allies across the globe," Mardequai continues. "It heartens me to share that our key partners are resolute in their commitment to proceed with our plan, regardless of the official theatrics that may unfold at the assembly."

"And who might these mysterious allies be?" inquires Catherine.

"We have secured the support of influential factions in Russia, Brazil, and South Africa, to name but a few," Mardequai replies smoothly. "As for those still wavering in their allegiance, I believe I have the perfect individual to sway their hearts and minds."

Orna arches a sceptical brow. "I sincerely hope

you're not referring to that impetuous foster child of yours, Mardequai."

Sofia grimaces instinctively at the mention of herself.

"While you may harbour reservations about Sofia, there is no denying her unique ability to connect with the younger generation," Mardequai counters, unruffled. "As I'm sure you'd agree, it would be remiss to overlook the fact that sixty-two percent of witches in Britain are under the age of thirty. They yearn for a voice that resonates with their disillusionment and aspirations, not merely as practitioners of magic, but as women in a world still mired in inequality."

"Why, Mardequai, I hadn't pegged you for a feminist," Catherine remarks with a note of surprise.

"Feminism has nothing to do with it. This is about harnessing the zeitgeist, about understanding the pulse of the rising generation. Sofia, for all her rough edges, has her finger firmly on that pulse. The influence someone like her could have among young witches is not something we can afford to ignore."

Sofia's mind races as she processes Mardequai's words. That much is true: she knows that simmering rage all too well – it burns in her own veins, a restless fire seeking kindling. Young witches like herself have long been chafing under the weight of ancient traditions. They're tired of being dismissed as impulsive and naïve, their ideas and hunger for change in the world usually met with condescension. At every turn, they find themselves stifled by the very institutions meant to nurture their potential.

"She doesn't know it, of course, but Sofia has been reared for this task," continues Mardequai. "It's been my intention all along to use her one day, when she is ready. One could say, she was born for it." At that, he and the other druids chuckle as if they know something the rest do not. "All it takes to spread a fire is one wild ember. Sofia is that ember – a catalyst for change, a spark to ignite the passions of her peers. Under my guiding hand, she will grow into a symbol of rebellion, of defiance against the status quo. Her very existence will be a rallying cry for the disaffected youth, a beacon for those who dream of a new order."

Catherine's voice cuts through the room like a whip. "You took her in and raised her only to use her as you see fit? What kind of a father are you?"

Mardequai's reply is as chilling as it is logical. "The kind that understands the necessity of sacrifice for the greater good. The kind who knows that sentiment has no place in the forging of destiny. Sofia's role has always been larger than herself, larger than any one individual. She is an instrument of change, a means to an end – and that end is none other than the salvation of our kind."

A stunned silence descends upon the gathering.

Out on the balcony, Sofia feels as if the very ground beneath her feet has turned to quicksand, threatening to swallow her whole. In the span of a few heartbeats, the façade of her life has shattered, ripped away to expose a cold reality. She grips Pippa's hand like a lifeline, a single, searing tear tracing a path down her cheek. Deep down, she has always known the truth, yet hearing it spoken aloud cuts her to the core.

Of course, she has never truly been a daughter to Mardequai. Their bond has always been one of convenience, a relationship devoid of genuine affection. But to learn that she's nothing more than a pawn in his grand scheme, a tool to be exploited at his whim?

The sting of that revelation is more than she can bear.

Four

The Range Rover speeds away from Cliveden House, an oppressive silence hanging between Pippa and Sofia. They waited until the ominous discussion concluded, but instead of meeting Mardequai as he requested, Sofia rushed back to the car, insisting that Pippa drive off immediately.

Now the rolling hills and lush countryside of Berkshire whizz by as they journey back to London. Green fields dotted with grazing sheep stretch out on either side of the winding road, the serenity of the landscape at odds with the tension inside the vehicle.

Pippa finally breaks the silence. "Are you going to say something, or should I?"

"It was just a kiss, Pippa. Don't freak out," Sofia

replies, fully aware that Pippa is referring to something else entirely.

"I'm not talking about the *kiss*," Pippa exclaims, gripping the steering wheel tighter. "They are planning to hold humans like pets! What do you have to say to that?"

"Actually, more like cattle when you think about it," Sofia responds. The thought of wiping Pippa's memory has crossed her mind since the moment they returned to the car, but she also longs for someone else in the know.

Pippa glances at Sofia through the rearview mirror. "Did... did you know about this? Is this why you've been stirring up trouble all summer? Because he asked you to?"

Sofia lets out a heavy sigh. "He did request that I make a name for myself, but I had no idea why. Until now."

"So, you just blindly follow his orders without question?" Pippa presses.

"Don't *you*?" Sofia snaps back. However, her voice softens as she continues, "We all do, Pippa. You, me, and every other minion on his payroll."

An uncomfortable silence settles between them once more. Finally, Pippa speaks up. "So, what are you going to do now?"

"I don't know, alright?" Sofia snarls. She closes her

eyes, taking a breath to compose herself. "I... I need to think. Can you just... drive? Take me anywhere you want, as long as it's not back to the city."

The two women spend the remainder of the afternoon and well into the night driving aimlessly, the silence between them heavy and unbroken. Pippa's eyes remain fixed on the road ahead, while Sofia's gaze wanders, lost in the changing landscape that passes by her window. As the hours tick by, the tension in the car grows.

Finally, Pippa brings the car to a stop atop a hill overlooking a cluster of villages nestled in the valley below. Distant streetlights twinkle below the darkening sky, a glimmer of civilisation amidst the vast expanse of the countryside.

"Where are we?" Sofia asks as she opens the car door. The humid night air envelops her, carrying with it the promise of a storm brewing on the horizon.

"Surrey Hills," Pippa replies. "I grew up here."

Sofia nods and steps out of the car, her feet carrying her towards the edge of the hill as if drawn by an invisible force. As she stands there, gazing out at the distant storm clouds, the occasional lightning strike illuminates the sky, casting an eerie glow across the landscape.

And maybe it's the serenity of this place, or maybe the childhood nostalgia wafting over from Pippa, but somehow this place stirs long-buried memories within her, too, transporting her back to the German countryside where she grew up. She has long made a habit to push these thoughts aside – clearly a coping mechanism to avoid confronting the pain that still lingers. However, in this moment, the memories of her loved ones surge forth, refusing to be ignored any longer.

Settling into the grass, Sofia begins to sing a melody – the lullaby that has been etched into her very being, and the one true comfort she always returns to.

The song holds a special meaning, one that extends far beyond herself, her family, her past. From the moment of their birth, the Hausmann twins were gifted with the ability to access fleeting glimpses of their past lives – a talent so rare that even among witches their parents never encountered another with such capabilities. They first discovered their daughters' access to past lives when Alva, Sofia's late twin, recounted harrowing experiences from a previous existence during World War II. The details she shared –names, places, dates – were so vivid, so precise that their parents were able to corroborate them with historical records, leaving no doubt about the authenticity of Alva's recollections.

In contrast, Sofia's own connection to the past has always been far more elusive. Nothing but fleeting glimpses, really. The sole memory she has ever managed to summon is that of an ailing witch who lived a solitary existence deep within some forest, secluded in a humble stone cottage. The old crone, her wild hair like a tangled bird's nest, rummaged around in her overgrown garden, her bony fingers plucking weeds and herbs. Every now and then, she would pause, squinting at a particularly stubborn weed, before letting out a triumphant "Aha!", then yanking it from the earth. The scene, both amusing and strangely endearing, never fails to move Sofia. The crone's voice, something between a cackle and a screech, forever carrying the very same lullaby that now flows from Sofia's lips:

Remember, remember, the stories of old,
The memories that slipped through your fingers like gold.
Let magic uncover what time tried to hide,
As the lost becomes found, with you by my side.

Remember, remember, the dreams that you hold,
The wonders inside you, waiting to unfold.
With each passing moment, each wish and each star,
Your song holds the key to where memories are.

Indeed, the song means so much to her that she tattooed the lines '*Remember, remember, the dreams that you hold'* across her collarbone. Those words have always served as a reminder to hold fast to her aspirations, to never lose sight of the visions that burn within her heart. Deep down, Sofia has always known she was meant for... *more*. But now, in the face of Mardequai's plan for her, the lyrics take on a new, more unsettling meaning.

Standing here, on the edge of the hill, Sofia can't help but feel a sense of unease. The conversation she overheard at Cliveden House plays over and over in her head, sending a chill down her spine. *All it takes to spread a fire is one wild ember...*

What did Mardequai mean when he said, 'One could say, she was born for it?'

Is it true? Is she meant to lead her fellow witches into a new age? The very thought of it fills her with exhilaration. But does she want it like *that*? The idea of dominion, of subjugating humans to the whims of the magical forces, feels wrong, and on a fundamental level.

Yet, as she gazes out at the storm brewing in the distance, Sofia can't deny the growing sense of frustration that has been building all around her for years. It's for that very reason she voted 'Yes' to the referendum. Clearly, something ought to be done. The world is changing – and fast – the delicate balance between magic and nature becoming increasingly strained because humanity has tipped the scale. Just like Catherine

Delargy, Sofia has been noticing that subtle shift for a while. On some days, balancing Anima is becoming more of a challenge, like stilling a flag in the wind. She has also seen it during the lectures at Chyulu, heard it in the frustrated conversations among fellow students. Did Mardequai sent her to the Academy for this reason? So she could bear witness to the impending crisis and be moulded into the leader he envisions?

As the first drops of rain begin to fall, she closes her eyes, letting the cool wash over her face. The storm is nearly upon her. But before she surrenders herself to the deluge, Sofia will need answers.

———

Back at the Belgravia mansion, Mardequai waits for Sofia in her bedroom. The window frames his silhouette, hands clasped at the small of his back – the age-old posture of those who wait and watch.

"I expected you at Cliveden House," he remarks, his gaze still fixed on the darkened gardens outside.

"Sorry, something came up."

Sofia doesn't expect to get away with the lie, but to her surprise, Mardequai allows it to hang in the air, uncontested. Yet, as he turns around and considers her, the unspoken truth settles between them like incense smoke: somehow, he knows she overheard the conversation at Cliveden. Perhaps he saw the Rover drive off, or maybe he can discern it from the subtle shifts in her expression. Sure enough, anyone who has lived this long would be adept at catching lies.

"What did you want to talk about, anyway?" Sofia enters the room and sits at her vanity, hugging one knee to her chest.

"The next steps, my dear. The path that lies ahead." Mardequai's eyes glint. "You have a vital role to play, Sofia. I truly meant that. Harness the power within you and you'll lead our kind into a whole new era."

So, he won't even mince words now, won't even pretend he doesn't know about her eavesdropping.

Sofia shifts uncomfortably. "But...so...what does that mean, exactly?"

"It means a fresh start, a clean slate for our community. When the assembly prepares the Reveal this autumn, we have an opportunity to reshape the world in our image, to ensure that our kind, witches and druids, finally seize the role meant for us." Mardequai's voice grows more fervent with each word.

"Why have we been in hiding for so long, anyway?" Sofia asks.

"Because we are a minority. A powerful one, but a minority nonetheless," replies Mardequai. "Didn't they teach you that at Chyulu? Nature always requires balance. There may be millions of zebras on the African steppe, but only a couple dozen lion prides. It was decided long ago that magic shall be hidden because, though powerful, the lions could not risk being trampled. Too valuable was their power, too important their wisdom – a decision, I believe, that has now reached its zenith. I stand with my esteemed colleagues who believe that something ought to change. Sadly, we disagree on the 'what.'"

Sofia hesitates, a flicker of doubt causing her eyes to narrow. "But you wouldn't want to, like... *hurt* anyone, would you?"

Mardequai smiles. Which might have been meant to be reassuring, but somehow entirely achieves the opposite. "My sweet child, I won't insult you with a lie: I've been in this world long enough to know that systematic change is never easy. I was there when the Black Death struck Europe in 1347, and when Napoleon lost at Waterloo in 1815. Of course, I warned him that underestimating the Duke of Wellington would be his downfall, but he refused to heed my advice," he adds, trailing off momentarily. "It is an ugly truth, but a universal one nonetheless: you cannot uproot the tree without disturbing the soil. But there's too much at stake to shy away from that responsibility. Mother Earth herself is calling us for help."

Sofia instinctively draws back, her head recoiling like a snail within its shell at that last statement. It feels oddly incongruous – something he'd say to persuade her rather than reflect his own convictions.

"And I'm sure you'd agree," he continues, "that there are also people who *deserve* to be punished. People who keep telling a story that belongs to the past." He gently nudges the edges of *The Sun* newspaper showing David Voss's enraged face. "The revelation of our existence to humans is imminent." Mardequai sighs. "But it would be naive of us to expect humans will embrace our kind with open arms. They are governed by fear; they always have been. They will inevitably fight against what they cannot comprehend, mark my words. And when that day comes, we best be ready."

"So, that's all it is, then?" Sophia asks, her eyes searching his. "A precautionary measure?"

"Indeed, a precautionary measure," Mardequai confirms, his gaze holding hers.

Sofia pauses for a long moment. Finally, she summons the courage to confront the question that has been burning in her mind, no matter if it revealed that she had been a bad girl.

"What did you mean when you said, I was born for it?" she brings forth, almost stumbling over the words.

Mardequai meets her gaze with that glint in his eyes, that flicker of disappointment. It's clear he would have preferred to maintain at least a sliver of pretence.

"I still remember the day I saved you all those years ago," he says at last. "You were lying in the grass at the side of the road. The burnt-out car. The smoke. Your small frame shivering, racked with the pain of your loss. The air so thick with smoke and your anguished cries..."

Instinctively, Sofia wraps her arms around herself, just as she did then.

"I took you under my protection that day. And from the moment I witnessed your magic, I knew how exceptional you are, how gifted. I believe, deep down, you recognise it, too." Mardequai turns to face her, his gaze intense. "You've always known that you have a pivotal role to play. We both do. Why else did you survive when your entire family perished? Why else was it I who came to save you? Can't you see? We are destined to achieve great things together, you and I. After countless centuries of observing history's cycles, watching eras rise and fall, if there's one truth I hold unshakable, it is that there is a profound purpose in the way life unfolds. There are no coincidences. You, Sofia," he says, his eyes boring into hers, "were born to be my ember."

There is no need to explain his metaphor further. At this point they both know she has heard it before. However, its poignant accuracy likely surpasses even Mardequai's understanding. The truth is, ever since the tragic day that car went up in smoke, taking the lives of those she loved most, a flame survived, an ember smouldering deep within Sofia's core. A seething rage, all-consuming, burning, threatening to devour her from the inside out unless she releases it. It's an insatiable desire she cannot explain, to embrace the darkest recesses of her being, to lose herself in the chaos she so desperately craves.

The truth is, stricken with grief and raised in isolation, Sofia has gone a little mad.

"And what would you have me do?" she asks at last.

Mardequai's gaze locks with hers, a flicker of satisfaction dancing in his eyes. "I need you to rally the youth behind you. Every swarm requires a queen, and young witches will gravitate towards your passion, your truth, even your rage. *Especially* your rage." He picks up the newspaper from the bed, then places it next to Sofia on her vanity. "I believe the time has come for you to seize control of your hive, wouldn't you agree?"

He turns to leave but pauses at the threshold. "You have identified your first adversary," he says, his voice low, purposeful. "Now bring about his downfall and make it a spectacle they'll never forget."

With that, Mardequai slips out of the room, leaving Sofia alone in the shadows. The dim glow of a nearby streetlamp spills through the window, its light falling across David Voss's photograph, standing before his Soho club.

After a silence that seems to stretch on for ages, Sofia finally opens the door, revealing – Pippa.

"So? What's happening?" Pippa asks and slips inside. "What are you going to do?"

Sofia meets her gaze. "I need you to call *The Sun* first thing in the morning. I'll give them an exclusive interview."

Pippa's eyes widen, a spark of hope igniting. "You're going to tell them then? You're going to do the right thing?"

Sofia turns towards her, features hardening as a shadow of regret passes over her face. "Not exactly."

Now Pippa's voice trembles. "You... You're not going to... Please tell me you're not going to follow through with his plan."

Sofia remains silent, her gaze drifting towards the window. She moves closer, opening it to allow the night air to flood the room. Outside, heavy rain patters against the sill. The storm has broken.

"Sofia? If you go through with this…" Pippa's voice breaks. "I swear, I will hate you forever."

Sofia turns back to face her. "No, you won't," she replies softly. The words carry a heaviness that seems to surpass their simple meaning.

"Wh… what are you saying?" Pippa's eyes fill with tears. Realisation seems to dawn on her then, and she takes a step back. "No, don't you dare. Don't you dare take my memories!" she warns, but Sofia has already raised a hand, poised to draw energy from the rain for the spell.

"It's better if you don't know," Sofia whispers, her own eyes brimming with unshed tears. "But I promise you, I will always keep you safe."

"*Fuck you*, Sofia." Now Pippa trembles with anger, tears streaming down her face as she shakes her head. "*Please*… please don't do this," she pleads. "You… you don't have to do any of this…"

But it's too late. The spell has already been cast, and in an instant, Pippa's expression shifts from one of outrage to a compliant smile.

"I will contact *The Sun* first thing in the morning," she says, her voice now devoid of any emotion. "Is there anything else you require for now?"

"No, that will be all," Sofia replies, her sombre

expression the sole remnant of the truth they shared mere moments ago. Pippa nods and excuses herself.

Sofia turns back toward the window and closes it, the storm now raging outside, raindrops pelting against the glass.

"Remember, remember, the dreams that you hold," she whispers, caressing her inked collarbone as her breath fogs up the glass. "...the wonders inside you... waiting... to unfold."

And in that moment, it is as if something fundamental has shifted within her – a hardening of resolve, a refining of purpose. She will play the role Mardequai assigned her, alright... but she will do so on her own terms.

And heaven help anyone who stands in her way.

FIVE

The Artesian at the Langham Hotel exudes an air of luxury and class. Purple velvet seating, gleaming marble surfaces, dazzling crystal chandeliers.

Lunch hour has drawn an array of visitors, business executives as well as discerning tourists, their conversations blending with the soft tinkling of ice in glasses and the gentle strains of Bossa Nova music.

Sofia makes her entrance clad in an off-the-shoulder Versace dress that perfectly showcases her brand-new tattoo of a twisting flame. The vivid pink of her dress immediately draws the eye and sets her apart from the rather dull sea of tailored suits and cocktail dresses. As she crosses the room, heads turn and murmurs of recognition spark like embers catching dry wood.

Sofia's eyes scan the room, finally landing on the booth where the journalist eagerly awaits her arrival. With a casual toss of her perfectly styled hair, she makes her way towards the table.

"Brad Schneider," the man introduces himself as he stands to greet her, his smile barely concealing his excitement at landing such a high-profile interview.

"Mypinkcauldron, I presume?"

"In the flesh."

As they slide into the booth, Brad wastes no time cutting to the chase. "So, your Instagram stories have been causing quite the stir lately. What made you decide to break your silence and agree to this exclusive?"

Sofia holds up a freshly manicured finger. "Hold that thought, darling. I'm going to need a drink before we dive into our juicy tale." She catches the eye of a waiter and beckons him over.

"I'll have a dirty martini, extra olives, and make it a double. Actually, we'll have two," she instructs. "Trust me, Brad, you're going to want one too once you hear what I have to say."

As the waiter hurries off to fulfil her order, Sofia leans back in her seat, crossing her legs.

"Now, where were we? Ah, yes, the reason behind this little tête-à-tête," she begins, her lips curling into a wicked grin. "Well, Brad, let's just say that a certain someone has been a thorn in my side for far too long, and it's high time I plucked it out, once and for all."

"I take it you're referring to David Voss?" Brad prods, pen poised above his notebook.

"Bingo," Sofia exclaims, snapping her fingers. "You see, not many people know this, but David and I go way back, and not in a good way."

Just then, the waiter arrives with the drinks, placing them carefully on the table. Sofia picks up the glass. She takes a slow sip, savouring the burn of the alcohol in her throat.

"What do you mean, exactly?" Brad inquires further, taking a sip of his own drink.

"Why, we used to be an item, darling."

Brad's eyes widen, his journalistic instincts kicking into fifth gear. "An ex-lover's quarrel turned public feud? This is juicy stuff, indeed. What caused the split?"

Sofia's expression darkens, her voice dropping to a whisper. "David's not the gentleman he portrays himself to be. Behind closed doors, he was a real piece of work. Controlling, manipulative, and not always gentle, if you know what I mean."

Brad scribbles away as if his life depends on it.

"He'd get handsy at parties," Sofia continues, "force

himself on me in private. It was a nightmare, but I was stupid to think I could change him."

Brad's face grows serious. "That must have been difficult. What finally gave you the strength to leave?"

Sofia takes a deep breath, her gaze growing distant as she recalls the pivotal moment Mia Bennett shared with her in confidence. Afraid she wouldn't be believed, Mia never reported the incident. "It was a night I'll never forget," Sofia says, recounting her friend's exact words. "I came home from a charity event to find David in a rage. He'd been going through my phone, convinced I was cheating on him. The accusations, the screaming... it was all too much. And when he raised his hand to me, I finally had enough."

She pauses, her fingers tracing her new shoulder tattoo, still swollen around the edges.

"I realised that if I didn't leave then, I might not make it out alive. So, I kicked his sorry ass goodbye and never looked back." Her eyes flash and she takes another sip of her drink. She reclines on the bench. "Naturally, David couldn't handle it. He's been out to destroy me ever since."

Brad nods, scribbling furiously. "And now you're ready to take the power back and expose him for the monster he truly is?"

Sofia grins. "Oh, honey, you have no idea. By the

time I'm done, David Voss won't know what hit him. This pink cauldron is about to boil over, and he's going to get burned."

Brad Schneider grins as he writes. "Can I quote you there?"

"You better," says Sofia. "And now if you'll excuse me, pet, I have a patriarchy to overthrow." With that, she gracefully slides out of the booth, just as the journalist asks his final question.

"And who would I be quoting, exactly?"

Sofia turns on her heel. Of course, she anticipated this. "You want a name?" she asks, eyes blazing.

"I want *your* name."

Sofia saunters closer to the table. Without breaking eye contact, she reaches for Brad's martini and raises it to her lips. In one smooth motion, she tosses back the remainder of the drink. "My name," she says, wiping the edges of her mouth with her thumb, "is Ember Wild."

"Amber Wild, is it?" Brad repeats, writing down the name.

"No, darling. It's Ember, with an *E*," Sofia corrects him.

"Ember? Is that a nickname or...?"

A slight smirk plays on her lips as she leans in, her presence palpable like the heat of a fire.

"You know what they say, Brad," she purrs. "All it takes to spread a fire is one wild ember."

And with those parting words, Ember Wild strides out of the Artesian, the ashes of Sofia Hausmann scattering in her wake.

The Sun Exclusive: Ember Wild Takes Down Voss Club Empire!

In a shocking turn of events, Ember Wild, the mysterious socialite and internet sensation formerly known as 'mypinkcauldron,' has single-handedly brought down the nightlife empire of David Voss. Wild courageously came forward a couple of weeks ago with accusations of sexual assault against the once-untouchable club mogul, providing compelling evidence in the form of images and video recordings to support her claims (as previously reported by The Sun*).*

Voss, in a desperate attempt to save face, insisted that the damning footage was nothing more than a sophisticated deep fake. However, his denials fell on deaf ears as several other women, emboldened by Wild's bravery, stepped forward with their own harrowing accounts of assault and harassment at the hands of the disgraced entrepreneur.

But just who is Ember Wild? In a tell-all interview with The Sun's *own Brad Schneider a few weeks ago, the long-debated identity of the elusive 'mypinkcauldron' was finally revealed. As previously rumoured, Ember Wild is none other than the daughter of Mardequai Guise, the notoriously reclusive tycoon at the helm of an elite art dealership network. Guise, rarely seen in public, is known for his extensive collection of priceless masterpieces and his influence in the upper echelons of society.*

As for Voss, he had no choice but to settle the lawsuit with Ember Wild, agreeing to her audacious demand: the transfer of ownership of all his nightclubs, including the legendary Sapphire Lounge, to the very woman who brought about his downfall.

In a stunning reversal of fortune, Ember Wild now sits atop the throne of London's nightlife scene, a queen rising from the ashes of her past trauma.

SIX

Ember stands tall and defiant in front of the Sapphire Lounge in the heart of Soho.

The London neighbourhood buzzes with energy; the air is thick with the mingled scents of street food, cigarette smoke, and the faint traces of spilled alcohol. Clad in skinny jeans and a bold, black T-shirt emblazoned with the words Fuck the Patriarchy, she raises her hand, extending her middle finger towards the smartphone, which Pippa holds up to film. At that very moment the sign of the Sapphire Lounge shatters to the ground in a satisfying crash of metal and glass. Ember turns and strides forward while Pippa continues to document her march on the club entrance.

Above them, a brand-new sign is being hoisted into

place: the words My Pink Cauldron gleam in neon pink. Ember pauses at the threshold of the club, a small smile playing at the corners of her lips before she steps inside. She wastes no time in sharing her triumph with her followers. A few quick taps on her phone and she has uploaded the video to Instagram. For a song, she chooses "Under Pressure" by Bowie and Queen. For a caption, she writes, "Your Queen has found a hive. Assemble at My Pink Cauldron, witches."

As the likes, comments, and shares begin to pour in, Ember passes through the plush, dimly lit interior. Pushing open the door of Voss's former office, she surveys the room. The space exudes an excess of masculine opulence: dark leather furniture, depressing mahogany surfaces, walls adorned with tasteless artwork.

All that will have to go, naturally.

Ember saunters over to the safe, which she opens with a flourish. Reaching into her pocket, she retrieves a memory stick – the one containing the original surveillance camera footage from the last time she entered this very room. She skilfully manipulated it, using her magic to frame Voss.

Behind the imposing desk that dominates the room, she settles into her new throne, draping her legs across the desk and reaching for her phone, eager to bask in the adulation of her fans. She scrolls through the comments and DMs that have flooded her account within seconds, her grin widening with each message of support, each declaration of allegiance to the new queen of Soho.

Pippa enters the office, a tablet clasped in her hands. "Elton John has RSVP'd to the relaunch party," she reports. "The Mandrake would like to offer you their penthouse free of charge as your permanent London residence, Mr Guise requests dinner at the townhouse tonight, and did you order a giant Free the Nipple sign by any chance? Because there's a deliverer at the door who needs you to sign for that."

"Fabulous." Ember unfolds her legs and rises in one fluid motion. "I'll be right out."

Pippa gives a curt nod, making a note on her tablet as she turns to leave. Ember casts one more glance at her phone, about to put it away, but a message catches her eye, causing her to freeze in place.

"I'll be just a minute, darling..."

She blinks, wondering if her eyes are playing tricks on her. Heart pounding, she sinks into the plush office chair. There, she stares at the phone in her hand, the room around her fading into a distant haze as a storm of emotions washes over her. All that exists in this moment is the message on the screen. She taps on it, fingers trembling, pulse quickening as she reads the words written in German:

Alva Hausmann: Sofia, bist du das?

...Sofia, is that you?

THANK YOU FOR READING, DARLING.

If you're itching to find out what happens next, book 1 in the series, THE FLAMES THAT FORGED US, is out now...

www.ingramcontent.com/pod-product-compliance
Lightning Source LLC
Chambersburg PA
CBHW021749190726
48290CB00008B/2544